This Book BiTES!

Or, Why Your Mouth Is More Than Just a Hole in Your Head

by Timothy Gower

Acknowledgments

I'd like to thank the following people for taking the time to mouth off about the oral cavity: Theodore P. Croll, D.D.S.; Clinton Detweiler; Charles C. Diggs, Ph.D.; Alan L. Felsenfeld, D.D.S.; Alan R. Hirsch, M.D.; and Lowan Han Stewart. I'm also indebted to published research on laughing and yawning by Robert Provine.

Dedication: This book is dedicated to my mother, who never washed my mouth out with soap.
—Timothy Gower

And Now a Message from Our Corporate Lawyer:

"Neither the Publisher nor the Author shall be liable for any damage that may be caused or sustained as a result of conducting any of the activities in this book without specifically following instructions, conducting the activities without proper supervision, or ignoring the cautions contained in the book."

The Planet Dexter Guarantee

If for any reason you are not satisfied with this book, please send a simple note telling us why (how else will we be able to make our future books better?!) along with the book to

The Editors of Planet Dexter
One Jacob Way, Reading, MA 01867-3999
e-mail us at pdexter@awl.com or visit us at
www.planetdexter.com

We'll read your note carefully, and send back to you a free copy of another Planet Dexter book. And we'll keep doing that until we find the perfect Planet Dexter book for you.

Cool, eh?

Text copyright © 1999 by Timothy Gower. All rights reserved. Published by Planet Dexter, a division of Penguin Putnam Books for Young Readers, New York. Published simultaneously in Canada. Printed in China.

ISBN 0-448-44081-4   A B C D E F G H I J

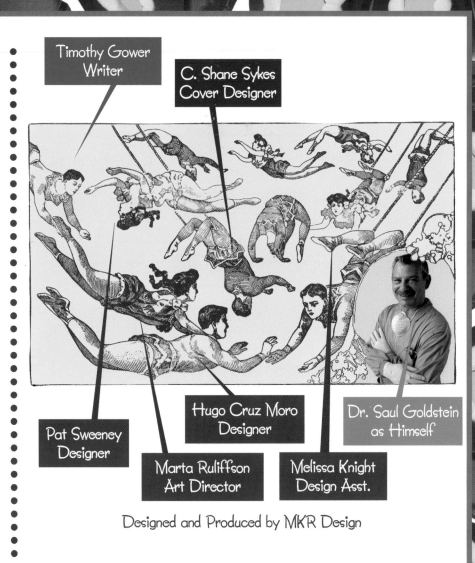

Timothy Gower
Writer

C. Shane Sykes
Cover Designer

Dr. Saul Goldstein
as Himself

Pat Sweeney
Designer

Marta Ruliffson
Art Director

Hugo Cruz Moro
Designer

Melissa Knight
Design Asst.

Designed and Produced by MKR Design

Library of Congress Cataloging-in-Publication Data

Gower, Tim.
   This book bites! : or, why your mouth is more than just a hole in your head / Tim Gower.
     p.   cm.
   Summary: Discusses all aspects of the mouth and its uses, importance, and phenomena, including teeth, cavities, hiccups, the tongue, spit, the mechanics of munching, yawning, and more.
   ISBN 0-448-44081-4
   1. Mouth—Juvenile literature. [1. Mouth.] I. Title.
QM306.G68   1999
611'.31—dc21   98-45431
                                      CIP
                                      AC

Why This Book Bites!

CONTENTS

Your Mouth:
Much More Than Just

AN INTRODUCTION

After all, you've got plenty of holes in your head. But none is as much fun as your mouth. Do you think for one minute that we'd bother to publish a book called *This Book Sniffs* or *This Book Has Ear Wax*?

No Way!

Those other holes in your head may be great for breathing and hearing, but go ahead and try using one to eat ice cream. Or gab on the phone. Or chew gum, scream

"Wake Up!!!"

in your little brother's ear when he's sound asleep, laugh, kiss … well, did we mention the part about eating ice cream? Your mouth (known to fancy-talking doctors as your "oral cavity") is one very amusing body part.

Heck, compared with your elbow or tibia or pancreas, your mouth is positively a barrel of laughs. It cracks jokes. It whistles. It makes funny noises when people bend over.

But your mouth is much more than a jokester. Life would be unlivable without your mouth. You couldn't talk (horrors!), eat (egad!), or drink (makes you thirsty just thinking about it, eh?). And your mouth performs all these vital tasks with a big, wide smile.

a Hole in Your Head!

It may be dark and damp inside your oral cavity, but *This Book Bites!* will make it less of a mystery. Read on and find out

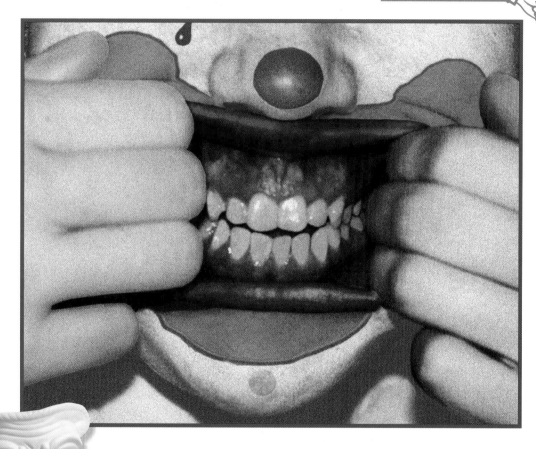

. . . why doctors make you say "ahhh."

. . . why your voice sounds so weird on tape.

. . . why people kiss.

. . . why you get the hiccups.

. . . why Michael Jordan sticks out his tongue when he leaps up to stuff a basketball. (Actually, nobody knows why he does that, but you'll learn all kinds of other cool stuff about tongues, like how yours has its own built-in sprinkler system for keeping your taste buds clean.)

There's lots more here for you to devour, so open wide.

A Few Tips About Lips

Item: Yer kisser

Fancy name doctors use: Labia (LAY bee uh).

QUANTITY: Two—one each, upper and lower.

DESCRIPTION: Lips open the mouth when you want to talk or eat. They keep it closed at important times, too—if not, your mouth would turn into a bug trap when you ride your bike.

We are simply dying to show you around inside the mouth. But first we have to get past the lips. And that's not as easy as it sounds.

The lips are gatekeepers for the mouth. If they don't open, nothing enters. And although they may not look it, your lips are quite strong. They're surrounded by a thick ring of muscle called the orbicularis oris (or BIK you lar iss OR iss). This muscle closes the mouth and puckers the lips, which is why orbicularis oris is often called the "kissing

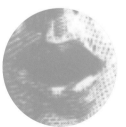

muscle." (Another reason it's called the kissing muscle is that saying "orbicularis oris" can get pretty tiring.)

Without your lips, food would fall out of your mouth while you eat, and we all know how unattractive *that* can be. The lips also help you form words when you speak. Plus, they come in very handy during kissing. More on that later.

Your lips form the meeting place between the dry skin of your face and the wet insides of your mouth. Unlike your skin, though, the outer part of your lips isn't kept moist by sebaceous glands (seh BAY shuss glanz), which supply oil. That's why lips become dried, or chapped, when they're exposed to too much sun or wind. When your lips become chapped, don't lick them! The spit on your tongue dries quickly and contains enzymes (EN zymz) that can make your lips hurt even more. You can avoid having chapped lips by using lip balm.

None of Your Friends Nose This One

You know that groove between your upper lip and the bottom of your nose? It has a name: the philtrum.

SCRATCH MY LIPS

In some parts of the United States, people used to say that if you have itchy lips it meant someone was saying bad things about you.

7

Lips are reddish because the skin covering them is relatively thin. That makes it easy to see the blood vessels under the surface. As you get older, the supply of blood that flows to your skin gradually decreases, so your lips lose some of their redness. This may explain the popularity of ...

LIPSTICK!

What's lipstick made of? Wax, mostly, with some oil from cow fat or other chemicals to make it shiny. The color comes from dyes.

AND SPEAKING OF DYES...

Most lipstick is red, of course, which is very bad news for a certain cactus-crawling critter. The red dye used in lipstick comes from the crushed shells of a stubby-legged bug found in the desert called the cochineal (koch uh NEEL) insect.

Come to think of it, that's not such great news for anyone who gets kissed by someone wearing lipstick. Speaking of smooches, read further to find out why we kiss in the first place.

Smack. Smooch.

And How to Be a Ventriloquist

Try this:

Your lips play an important role in speech. That's why ventriloquism is so difficult. Ventriloquists talk without moving their lips to create the illusion that their puppets are doing the chattering. That makes pronouncing letters that require lip movement—especially P, B, M, F, and V—a great challenge.

It takes years of practice to learn how to fool people, but here's one trick ventriloquists use. Without moving your lips, try saying, "peanut butter." Impossible, right? Say it again, but this time replace the "P" with a "K" and the "B" with a "G." Did you need to move your lips?

You're probably wondering: What the heck is "keanut gutter"? We don't know either. But when a ventriloquist says it really fast, in the middle of a sentence, using a funny voice, the listener "hears" the puppet say the words "peanut butter."

Lipless Life

What if humans didn't have lips? What if, instead, we had beaks?

- Women's magazines would be filled with ads for beak buffer.

- Noisy eaters would be told to quit snapping their beaks.

- The artist Rodin's famous sculpture "The Kiss" would have been named "The Peck."

- Catchers' masks would be a nightmare.

- Mothers would warn fresh-mouthed children not to give them any beak.

- Hickeys would really hurt.

9

Gross Moments

Or, The Disgusting Origins of Big Wet Ones

A KISS IS (NOT ALWAYS) JUST A KISS

There are many kinds of kisses, and just as many words and phrases for the act of kissing, including: BUSS peck

make out kissie-poo

Osculate smooch

give mouth-to-mouth

smack

play post office put him (or her) in a liplock

neck suck face

swap spit

Did we miss any good ones? Let us know.

The kiss is a universal sign of affection. No one knows for sure why people show that they like each other by puckering up and planting their lips on each other. But one of the main theories is a real gagger, so get in the mood for some pre-chewed food.

We're not kidding. Some scientists think that kissing all began with baby food.

Since babies don't have teeth, they can't chew food. That's why mothers feed them that mush that comes in little jars. Well, in the old days there was no mushy baby food—so mothers had to pre-chew food for their babies. After they got the food all soft and gooey in their own mouths—this is the gross part—they put their lips against their baby's mouth *and spit the food in.*

Since moms and babies would obviously have to be very fond of each other to perform this rather nauseating act, pressing lips together became known as a sign of love.

in Kiss-Tory

Kissin' Critters

A Little Lip Lore from the Animal Kingdom

Humans aren't the only creatures who kiss. But that doesn't necessarily mean everything is lovey-dovey when beasts buss each other.

The fish known as gouramis (goo RA mee) are also called "kissing fish." When two gouramis meet, they swim right up to each other and smack!—they kiss, for a long time, sometimes for hours. Scientists think, though, that the kiss isn't meant to be a sweet, tender greeting. It's a fight! The long kiss is one gourami's way of telling the other, "This is my turf—beat it!"

Sometimes, though, when a boy gourami and a girl gourami fight-kiss, they end up liking each other. So at least the story has a "happily ever after" ending.

Prairie dogs have even weirder kissing habits. When two meet, one walks right up and plants a peck on the other's cheek. This kiss helps the prairie dogs tell if they belong to the same clan. If they do, one picks dirt and bugs out of the other's fur, which is considered a very nice thing to do among prairie dogs. If they realize they come from different clans, a fight breaks out.

Kissing bugs don't smooch each other. But they do bite humans, often near the mouth, which is how they got their name. Kissing bugs are not trying to be friendly, though. They are also known as assassin bugs, and their bites hurt like heck, and they suck blood, and spread a disease that can harm your heart.

HOW 'BOUT A LOUD WET ONE, PAL?

In many parts of Europe, people greet each other with a kiss on the cheek. But in the French countryside, people used to believe that you could tell how much someone liked you by how loud they kissed your cheek. A noisy smack meant you were good friends.

Tooth Truths

Sink Your Teeth into This

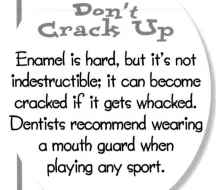

Don't Crack Up

Enamel is hard, but it's not indestructible; it can become cracked if it gets whacked. Dentists recommend wearing a mouth guard when playing any sport.

Item: Yer choppers

Fancy name dentists use: Dentition (den TISH un).

QUANTITY: Humans have twenty teeth by about age five, but before you can say "tooth fairy," they start falling out, one by one. Which is OK! That's because they're being pushed out by a new set, plus a dozen more. And that's good, since you need more teeth to fill out your growing mouth. If you end up with lots more than thirty-two teeth, you may be a dog or possibly a horse.

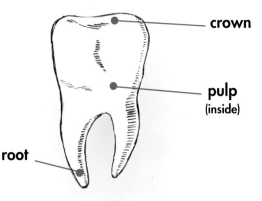

crown

pulp (inside)

root

DESCRIPTION: Crowns of teeth are rugged pegs that grow out of your jaws. They're ideal for ripping, cutting, and pulverizing things—preferably food. (Prehistoric humans used teeth as weapons, but today that's considered very bad taste.)

Teeth are covered with **enamel** (ee NAM ull)—the hardest stuff in your entire body. Underneath, the tooth is mostly made of **dentin**, a substance kind of like bone. The core of a tooth is filled with blood vessels and nerves: a big tangled mess known as the **pulp**.

Quick—how is a tooth like an iceberg?

Sorry, no riddle here. Most of an iceberg (as much as six-sevenths) is hidden below the surface of the water. Likewise, a big part of each tooth is buried in your gums— between one-half and two-thirds is invisible.

The visible part of a tooth is called the crown. The part buried is known as the root. The root is covered by bone-like stuff called **cementum**.

Meet the Chopper Squad!

Here's the crew of thirty-two that helps you bite and chew.

INCISOR

Nickname: "The Surgeon"
Profile: A real show-off, always pushing its way to the front. Blade-like edge; excels at cutting.
Quantity: Eight

CANINE

Nickname: "Fang"
Profile: A dogged tooth. Pointiest head in the bunch. Skilled at shredding and tearing.
Quantity: Four

PREMOLAR

Nickname: "The Handyman"
Profile: Multi-talented; helps canines with chopping and assists molars with grinding.
Quantity: Eight

MOLAR

Nickname: "Crusher"
Profile: Shy—tends to hide in the rear. A ruthless brute, nonetheless. Pounds, mashes, and grinds food into mush so it can be swallowed.
Quantity: Twelve

This crew can take a lot of abuse—but it has an arch enemy. Turn the page to meet this fiend.

BE FAIRIE TRUTHFUL

In some families, parents enjoy lying to their young children, telling them that there's a "tooth fairy" who will come in the middle of the night and leave a gift in place of any baby tooth placed under the child's pillow. Seriously, parents often create this "upside" for kids too young to read *This Book Bites!* and who are truly frightened by pieces of their bodies falling from their mouth. Think about it. Weird and scary, right?—It sure pays to read and understand.

Attack of the Killer Plaque!!!
Your Mouth's Very Own Slimy Crud

AARRRRGH! I WANT TO DESTROY YOUR TEETH!

Okay, so maybe plaque (PLAK) won't kill you. But it's still scary stuff. Plaque can destroy teeth the way Godzilla stomped on Tokyo. Except plaque is even creepier, because it's invisible!

That is, until you have so much that it accumulates and turns into a gooey white mess. Plaque starts off, though, as clear, slimy crud that sticks to your teeth. It's made of spit, little bits of food, and certain types of bacteria. The nastiest kind of bacteria that clings to your teeth is called *Streptococcus mutans* (strep TUHKOK kuss MEW tanz), known as *S. mutans*, for short.

S. mutans mixes with food to make a nasty acid. The acid eats away at the enamel on the outside of a tooth. Soon, a tiny hole forms on the tooth—you know this hole as the dreaded "cavity." But the hole isn't the *whole* problem, you might say. The real trouble starts when bacteria slimes its way into the cavity and infects the pulp of the tooth. This infection, known by the scientific name dental caries (CAYR eez), is what causes tooth decay.

First, the bad news: as you already know, *S. mutans* can't cause tooth decay alone. There must be food particles in your mouth. *S. mutans* especially loves foods that contain carbohydrates. "Carbos" are compounds found in many foods, such as pastas, fruits, and vegetables. Carbohydrates are an important part of the human diet: they give us energy.

Did we mention that sugar is a type of carbohydrate? Unfortunately, many wonderful sweet treats are filled with sugar. This is why eating entire five-pound boxes of candy and not brushing can cause tooth decay. And why parents are likely to sneak up behind you on Halloween night while you're quietly munching on a candy bar and scream,

"You better brush when you're done with that little vampire, or your teeth are gonna rot right out of your head!!!"

Now, the good news: When you brush your teeth, S. *mutans* heads for the hills. If you really slack off and don't brush for a long time, though, as many as one billion squirmy, microscopic bacteria can form on each tooth! But after you brush your teeth, the number drops way down—to as low as one thousand bacteria per tooth. When the number of little S. *mutans* beasties in your mouth is that low, they can't cause much trouble.

What happens if I forget to brush for, like, a week?

In a word, don't. When plaque stays on your teeth too long it can pick up minerals in your saliva and form dental tartar. Dentists call a deposit of tartar a "calculus," which (like the high school math class of the same name) is *really hard*. You can brush until your arm is ready to fall off and it won't remove a dental calculus. A dentist has to scrrrrrrape it off. There are much better ways to spend an afternoon, trust us.

So for healthy, happy teeth . . .
- Brush after every meal or snack, before going to bed, and when you wake up.
- At least once a day, preferably at bed time, floss before brushing your teeth.
- Swish around some fluoride rinse in your mouth once a day (be sure to spit it out).

HA! HA! HA! I CAN'T WAIT TO SCRRRRRRRAPE IT ALL OFF!!!

The Cavity

What to Say When You've Got Decay

LOOK MA! MY TEETH ARE FALLING OUT!

When your dentist says that you've got some tooth decay, parents often act as though you've done something awful, like you just robbed a bank or flunked history. So when they get on your case, simply recite these four important facts:

It's not like you INVENTED cavities. Anthropologists have dug up skulls of CroMagnon humans that show that some of our prehistoric ancestors had rotten teeth.

You are not alone. Not even close. Tooth decay is the most widespread health problem in the world, after the common cold.

You probably have fewer cavities than THEY did. When your parents were growing up, only one out of three children had no cavities. Today, fully half of all kids have no cavities. The biggest reason is that many communities today add a natural cavity-fighting element called **fluoride** (FLOOR eyed) to their water systems. Scientists think fluoride strengthens a tooth's enamel and may even weaken the acid produced by the S. *mutans* bacteria. If your town has fluoride in its water, just drinking a glass of water helps wipe out tooth decay. . . .

It's their fault you have cavities! It's true! After all, you were born with a clean and spotless mouth. But that didn't last long. When you were a baby your mother and father got in your face and made goo-goo noises. And whenever they did, little bits of spit flew out of their mouths and right into yours.

Try Worming Your Way Out of This One

Until the 1700s, many dentists believed that tooth decay was caused by worms.

Defense

Well, all that spit contained the dreaded *S. mutans* bacteria, which quickly made your mouth its permanent home and eventually caused you to develop tooth decay. So tell your parents: "I wouldn't have any cavities if you only knew how to **SAY IT—DON'T SPRAY IT!!!!**"

Why do they call them "wisdom" teeth?

The truth is, the third molars are called "wisdom" teeth because in most people they appear between the ages of 17 and 25—a time when people are supposed to be gaining the wisdom of adulthood. In some people, wisdom teeth grow in just fine. In others, wisdom teeth never appear, and it's no big deal. In many unlucky people, though, wisdom teeth get stuck in their jaws, but try to push their way out. And that hurts, so you have to have an operation to remove them.

Because, they really smart if they don't grow in right. (Har-dee-har-har!)

$E = MC^2?$

Welcome to the Gap!

If you've got a space between your two front teeth, you can tell your friends that you are "diastematic" (die uh STEE mat tick). Politely point out that the Swiss believe that a wide space between your teeth means that you'll be a great singer. And that a lot of famous people are gap-tooth types, too, including. . .

- Muhammed Ali, boxer
- Sandra Bernhard, actress
- Jimmy Carter, former president
- Dave Foley, actor
- Ron Howard, actor and director
- Samuel L. Jackson, actor
- Woody Harrelson, actor
- Lauren Hutton, actress and model
- David Letterman, talk show host
- Madonna, pop singer and actress
- Arnold Schwarznegger, actor and big strong guy
- Ben Stiller, actor
- Tom Watson, golfer

Brushing

A Far Better Option than the Nickname "Gummy"

SMACK!
SMACK!

#1 Just as you always wipe your boots off after a tour of Uncle Harry's hog farm or scrub your hands after changing Nephew Nort's diaper, you brush your mouth to rid it of all the really gross stuff that gets in there during normal use. Stuff like:

- the persistent remains of yesterday's Whopper-with-cheese
- microscopic traces of healthy squash and wheat germ snuck in there by parents
- pencil eraser crumbs from this morning's math class and
- nasal drippings

#2 Brushing massages your gums and that's a healthy thing (also, unlike when it comes to your neck or shoulders, you'll rarely find a friend or family member to massage your gums—yuck!).

The Seven Steps to Get-Lots-of-Hot-Dates Brushing

1. Place the head of the toothbrush alongside your teeth, with the bristle tips angled against the gum line. (By the way, if at this point you're in a dark room and/or not looking in a mirror and/or there's no toothpaste on the brush, we're outta here!)

2. Now move the brush back and forth with short strokes, in a gentle scrubbing motion. Brush one or two teeth at a time and then move on.

3. So that you don't forget any of your teeth, brush in quarters, continuing with the same short, back-and-forth strokes. One quarter is top-teeth-and-outside;

another is top-teeth-and-inside; then bottom-teeth-and-outside; and lastly, bottom-teeth-and-inside.

4. To brush the inside of the front teeth, hold the brush vertically, angle the bristles toward your gums, and use short up-and-down strokes.

5. To brush the chewing surfaces, keep the brush flat, and scrub out the pits and grooves of your molars.

6. Brush your tongue (try not to giggle!) and then rinse.

7. Feel free to stand real close to your loved ones.

The world's best brushers use a soft toothbrush and gentle pressure. The world's worst brushers use a discarded garden rack attached to the engine of a '68 Ford pickup truck.

Hiccups

When Your Mouth's Machinery Goes Amuck

What causes hiccups? They occur when you eat fish that's infested with tadpoles. In your stomach, the tadpoles mature into toads, whose loud "ribbits" come out of your mouth sounding like "hiccup."

JUST KIDDING!

Hiccups are actually caused by an irritation to the nerves that connect your brain and a muscle in your chest called the diaphragm (DIE uh fram). When you breathe normally, the fibers in the diaphragm slowly pull together, or contract. Hiccups happen when your brain sends a signal to the diaphragm to contract abruptly. But as air tries to rush into your chest, your vocal folds close, blocking the airway. Result: you make a very froggy sound.

Hiccups usually go away by themselves, but sometimes they can be a real nuisance. (A man in Iowa hiccuped for 69 years.)

Here are some possible cures for hiccups, suggested by real doctors:

- Hold your breath. When you exhale, you release carbon dioxide; holding your breath keeps carbon dioxide in your blood stream, which seems to stop hiccups.
- Breath in and out of a paper bag. (Do NOT put the bag over your head! If you do, hiccups will be the least of your worries.)
- Drink a glass of water quickly.
- Eat crushed ice.
- Eat bread.
- Eat one teaspoon of sugar.
- Ask someone to scare you. A good gasp interrupts the signal from your brain to diaphragm.
- Let out a belch.

RIBBIT

RIBBIT

RIBBIT

RIBBIT

IT'S NOT—
HIC!—FAIR!
Boys get hiccups more often than girls.

19

The Tongue

Worth More Than a Lick and How to Stare at It

Item: Yer lapper

Fancy name doctors use: Tongue (they must have run out of big words).

QUANTITY: One (if you have more than one tongue, you are either a space alien or a serious freak of nature).

DESCRIPTION: A pink muscle that morphs into all kinds of shapes, depending on the task.

Your tongue is one hard-toiling tool. You need it for talking and for swishing food around while you eat. But most of all, we think of the tongue as our taster.

Go to a mirror and stick out your tongue. (You have our permission.) Get really close. (If you're a heavy-duty mouth-breather, try not to steam up the glass.) See the little bumps on your tongue? They're called papillae (puh PILL ee). Papillae are *not* taste buds, like a lot of people think. Taste buds are much, much tinier and live *inside* the papillae. And taste buds aren't just found on your tongue, either. You've also got them in your throat and on the roof of your mouth. In fact, another word for the roof of your mouth is palate (PAL ett)— a word that can also mean "sense of taste."

When a taste bud absorbs a particle of food, it sends a message to your brain along nerves, telling whether the food is sweet (like candy), sour (like lemons), salty (like potato chips), or bitter (like swiss chard and certain other green, leafy vegetables). The cells that make up taste buds are replaced every 10 days. After you taste something, the buds get rinsed off by glands

papillae

THE BUD-DY SYSTEM

The average mouth has about 10,000 taste buds.

located between the papillae, so you can taste something else.

Some tongues are better at tasting than others, probably because they have more buds. Scientists call people with lots of taste buds "supertasters." Girls are more likely than boys to be supertasters. They're especially good at detecting sweet and bitter tastes.

A tasty tale, but not the whole story. Your taste buds only tell you a tiny bit about the flavor of food, believe it or not. Your brain gets most of its information about how a food tastes from a surprising source: **your nose.**

You might be thinking: Hold on just a minute. Except for that one time in kindergarten when I stuck some peas up there, I have NEVER *tried to eat with my nose! You gotta be kidding me!*

Of course you don't eat with your nose. But munching on food sends aromas upward, into your nasal (NAY zull) cavity, which is the space behind your nose. Special scent detectors in the nasal cavity send signals to the brain. But the brain thinks these *smells* are actually *tastes.*

Think we're joking? Jump to the next page and try a little experiment....

A Tongue-Lashing Would Have Sufficed, Thank You.

In ancient Mexico, religious people used to punish themselves for their sins by pulling strings of thorns through their tongues.

The Great Chocolate

Science Can Be Fun—and Delicious

HA! You probably thought we were going to pull the old apple-and-onion routine your science teacher has already shown you. If you haven't seen it yet, you probably will. In that experiment, your teacher shows you how your nose "tastes" food by tricking you into thinking that an onion is an apple. (Aren't science teachers just a barrel of laughs?) This experiment is the same idea, only more fun.

What to do: First, place the clothespin on your nose. If you don't have one (a clothespin, that is), just pinch your nostrils shut. Now take a bite of a chocolate bar. Notice that the candy feels soft and gooey on your tongue, but that the chocolate doesn't taste as rich and deep and all-around chocolatey as it should.

Now take off that silly clothespin, which was probably beginning to

WHAT YOU NEED:

ONE CHOCOLATE BAR

CHOCOLOCO

22

hurt, anyway. Take another bite of chocolate. Notice something? The flavor is much more interesting. It's more . . . chocolatey, don't you think?

What happened? Have you ever noticed that food doesn't taste as good when you have a stuffed-up nose? The same thing happened in this experiment. When you had the clothespin on your nose, no air was able to move in and out of your nasal cavity. That kept the delicious chocolate aroma from wafting up there. The powerful flavor detectors in your nose were pretty much shut off, leaving only the weaker taste buds in your mouth to do all the work of telling you how the chocolate tasted. And they didn't do a very good job, did they?

Cleanup: Dispose of remaining chocolate by mastication and deglutition (translation: munch and swallow). And don't forget to brush your teeth.

ONE MOUTH
(preferably your own)

ONE CLOTHESPIN

What Is the Sound of No Hands Clapping? Australian aborigines applaud by smacking their tongues.

More Fun with Tongues

Meaningful Minutia About The Muscle In Your Mouth

FINDING YOUR WAY AROUND A TONGUE MAP

Each part of your tongue can detect any taste, but some sections are better at detecting certain tastes than others. A map of the tongue might look like this:

TRY THIS:

Sprinkle a bit of sugar on the back of your tongue. Swallow it quickly. Now put another tiny bit of sugar on the tip of your tongue, then swallow. Which bit tasted more sugary?

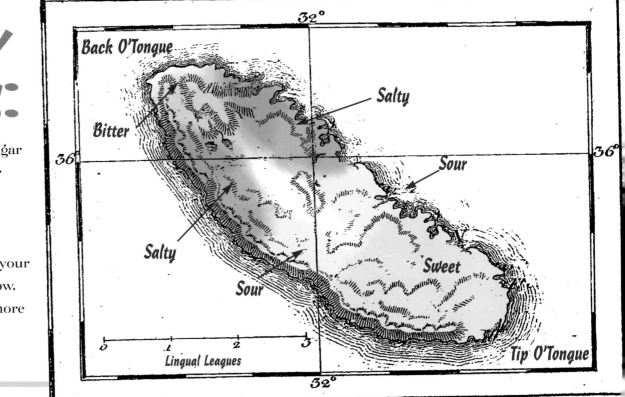

32°

Back O'Tongue

Salty

Bitter

36°   36°

Sour

Salty

Sweet

Sour

Tip O'Tongue

0   1   2   3

Lingual Leagues

32°

24

"TONGUE-TIED" UNRAVELING THE TRUTH ABOUT THIS KNOTTY CONDITION

Has anyone ever called you "tongue-tied" when you couldn't think what to say? Next time that happens speak up—and say that "tongue-tied" happens to be an actual medical condition, which doctors call **ankyloglossia** (ang kill o GLOSS ee uh). There's a piece of flesh in your mouth called the **frenulum** (FREN you lum) that attaches your tongue to the floor of your mouth. People who are born with very short frenulums have a hard time talking, since their tongues can't move freely. Fortunately, a surgeon can fix this problem by cutting away part of the frenulum. This unties the tied-up tongue.

A Taste for Battle

Sticking out your tongue to make fun of someone may have begun with ancient Greek warriors, who wagged their tongues at enemies to show they were thirsty for blood.

Roll out the Red ...Tongues?

Can You Roll Your Tongue? If You're Not Sure...

Try this:

Look in a mirror and stick out your tongue. Without touching it, try curling up the sides so your tongue forms a "U." Can you do it?

About two out of every three people can roll their tongues without making any special effort; everyone else is a flat-tongued type.

Many schools teach that you inherit the ability to roll your tongue from your parents. They say you are either a tongue-roller or you're not.

BUT THAT'S NOT TRUE!

Qualities that your parents pass down are called inherited traits. A well-known inherited trait concerns ear lobes. Some people have ear lobes that hang loose; others have ear lobes that attach to their head.

But the scientist who first claimed that tongue-rolling is an inherited trait later realized that this wasn't always true. One way he could tell was that some people can teach themselves to roll their tongues. Another scientist asked a bunch of identical twins to stick out their tongues. In some sets there was both a tongue-roller and a flat-tongued type. Identical twins inherit the exact same traits from their parents, so how could one be a tongue-roller and the other a flat-tongue? Scientists now believe that some—but not all—tongue-rollers get their talent from their parents.

If you're a flat-tongued type, don't feel left out: You may be able to teach yourself to roll your tongue. (Just don't expect any hearty congratulations if you do.)

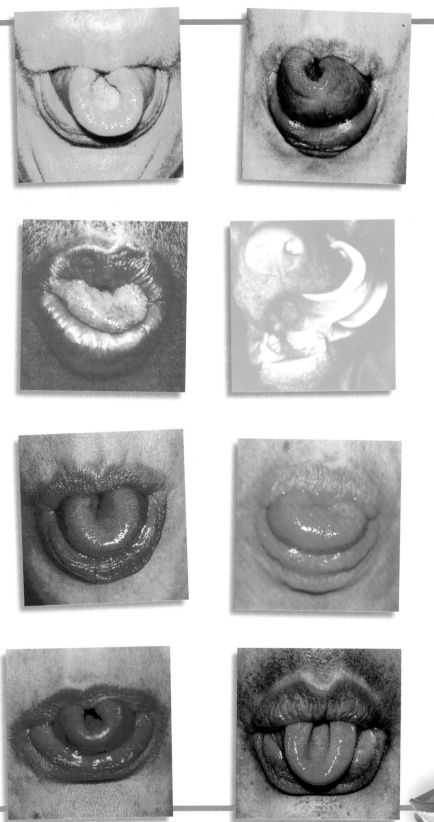

Hey! How's the Weather in There?

The Temperature In Your Mouth

When a doctor examines you, one of the first things he or she does is figure out your body temperature. And the easiest way to do that is to pop a thermometer in your mouth.

The inside of your mouth may not feel hot and sweaty, but if you took a vacation in there, you'd certainly want to pack a pair of shorts. You may have heard that the normal body temperature for a human is 98.6 degrees Fahrenheit. That's true, but it doesn't necessarily mean you're ready to keel over if your temperature is higher or lower. Here's how to prove that your body temperature changes throughout the day:

What you need: An oral thermometer and a watch or clock.

Ask one of your parents if he or she will help you take your temperature with the oral thermometer. (You can use either a digital type, which is like a tiny computer, or a clinical thermometer, which is the kind filled with mercury—both work just fine.) Take your temperature twice in one day: once before you eat breakfast and again right before dinner. Be sure not to eat or drink anything for a few minutes beforehand.

Compare the first temperature with the second. Was one higher than the other? Why do you suppose that happened?

Here's why: While you sleep, your muscles and bones barely do any work, so they give off very little heat. But a day of activity warms your body. Eating produces body heat, too. If your body temperature, as measured under your tongue, goes above 100 degrees and stays there, though, that's absolutely not normal. You have a fever and need to see a doctor.

Brush Your Tongue!

BAD BREATH EXPLAINED

Most smelly breath is caused by our old enemy dental plaque, which accumulates in your mouth if you don't brush frequently. To be sure you wipe out all the stink-causing plaque every time you brush, be sure to clean your tongue, especially the part toward the back of your mouth. (But don't make yourself gag!)

Mouthwash and mints can hide foul breath, but only for a short time. Some cases of bad breath can't be covered up at all, though. Certain foods, like garlic and onions, break down into a form of sulfur in your body. These smelly sulfur compounds are absorbed into your blood, which is pumped to your lungs. Then, when you exhale, your friends catch a whiff of a very funky stench. If you're having dinner with other people who are eating garlic and onions, no one will notice your bad breath. Otherwise, if you don't want to foul the air, you have two choices: either don't eat garlic and onions, or hold your breath after you eat (not recommended).

A HOT CONVERTIBLE

Some thermometers give the temperature in Celsius. To convert a Celsius temperature to Fahrenheit, multiply the number by 1.8, then add 32.

Spit Shines

High Praise For a Misunderstood Fluid

Spit, also known as **saliva** (suh LIE vah), has a lousy reputation. It wasn't always so bad, though. Up until the late 1800s in the United States, it was common to spit on the floor in factories and shops.

But when people began developing a deadly disease called **tuberculosis** (too berk you LOW siss), many cities passed laws forbidding spitting in public. Tuberculosis is spread through germs that float around in the air. Health officials feared that people who went around spitting might place others in danger of catching the dreaded disease.

Today, tuberculosis is less common, and most people's saliva is harmless, unless it gets into another person's bloodstream. But spitting is considered very bad manners; one of the rudest things you can do in our culture is spit on someone.

That doesn't mean saliva itself is a bad thing: Actually, it makes your mouth a much nicer place. Without saliva:

● Lips, tongue, cheeks, and everything else inside of your mouth would become as dry and cracked as the desert floor. (There's an illness known as **Sjögren's syndrome** [SHOW grenz SIN drohm] that causes people to have super-dry mouths and eyes.)

● You'd have more tooth decay, since spit helps wash bacteria out of your mouth.

● Food wouldn't taste so great, since the taste buds can only absorb food particles after saliva has helped dissolve them.

● Your stomach might hurt after you eat, since spit helps digest food.

● In fact, spit even helps cure one of the most dreaded afflictions known to humankind. . . .

MORNING BREATH!

You may have noticed that other people's breath doesn't smell so daisy-fresh when they first wake up in the morning. That's because our mouths make very little spit while we sleep. Saliva comes from several different pumps called **glands** in your mouth. But those glands take a long break while you sleep. Meanwhile, the bad-news bacteria in your mouth never rest. They just keep growing out of control, since there's nothing to wash them out of your mouth. And that bacteria

STINKS.

Don't worry, though. Once you brush your teeth or simply eat breakfast, your glands start making saliva again. And the air is once again safe to breathe.

Talk About Backwash!

The next time you see a one-liter bottle of soda pop, stop and think about this for a moment: in a single day, the average person's mouth produces enough saliva to fill that bottle (heavy-duty spit-makers can fill two).

spit

Contents: Water, amylase, mucin, urea, sodium, potassium, calcium, chloride, white blood cells, and tiny bits of debris from the lining of your mouth.

One liter

DROOL IN THE POOL

A FUN SPIT ACTIVITY!

What you need: A paper and pen (or a calculator), a good imagination.

We know that the average person's mouth produces one liter of spit each day. Imagine an Olympic-sized pool, which takes 1,891,763 liters of water to fill. If 100 people did nothing but spit in the pool all day and night, how long would it take them to fill it with saliva?

No Wonder Ye Olde Feet Are Wet

During the Middle Ages, it was perfectly okay to spit at the dinner table, as long as you did it under the table.

100 people would produce 100 liters of saliva each day. Since there are 365 days in a year, that would mean they produced 36,500 liters of saliva per year.

Do the math:

1,891,763 liters ÷ 36,500 liters = 51.8 years.

By which time those 100 people would probably have a really bad case of dry mouth.

Praise The Lord—Patooey!

Followers of some religions honor statues of their gods by spitting on them.

33

A Few Things Your Mouth Can Do Without

Did you ever look waaaaaaay in the back of your mouth and wonder: Hey! What is that thing, anyway? That little pink nubbin is your uvula (YOU view lah). It's about an inch long and shaped kind of like a punching bag. The uvula hangs down from the roof of your mouth and does very, very little else. You don't need it and you wouldn't miss it if one night your uvula quietly packed its bags, crawled out of your mouth, and moved to Pittsburgh.

Pittsburgh?

In fact, some people who snore when they sleep have their uvulas cut in half by a doctor. That's because they have floppy uvulas. While they snooze, the breeze coming out of their windpipes makes the uvula flap around in the back of their mouths. All that flapping makes an awful racket—kind of like a saw cutting through a log. Once the uvula has been trimmed, they snore no more.

Your **tonsils** aren't quite as useless as your uvula, but you still don't need them—at least not forever. Your tonsils actually form a ring, but the main parts are two hunks of flesh on either side of the back of your mouth. The uvula is one of their neighbors.

The tonsils help fight off infections, like the ones that cause common colds. They're like guard dogs for your throat. They attack nasty bacteria before they can slip down your gullet and make you sick. Unfortunately, sometimes the guard dogs themselves get sick from fighting all that bacteria and you develop an illness called **tonsillitis** (tawn sill EYE tiss). If you've already had it, you probably haven't forgotten.

When you have tonsillitis it KILLS to swallow anything.

A long time ago (that is, back when your parents were your age), kids who were always getting tonsillitis had to have their tonsils snipped out by a doctor. This hurt a lot, but as a reward, they got to eat ice cream for breakfast, lunch, and dinner. Which doesn't sound like such a bad deal, does it? Today, most bad cases of tonsillitis can be treated with medicine.

If you haven't had tonsillitis by now, there's a good chance you never will. That's because after about age nine or ten your tonsils shrink or disappear. They just shrivel up and go bye-bye. But you don't miss them, because your body doesn't seem to need them anymore. That may be because kids don't get as many infections as they get older.

Care for a Mint, Junior?

Sometimes food particles can get stuck in the crevices in tonsils. The food bits harden into putrid-smelling little white globs called tonsilloliths. If you've noticed these little nasties in your mouth, ask your dentist what to do about them.

35

Yadda Yadda Blah
Your Voice and How You Talk the Talk

When you speak, your mouth gets all the credit. But it does only part of the work. Every sound you make, from a whisper to a scream, begins in your chest—your lungs, to be precise. As you talk, your lungs push air out through your windpipe and into your voice box, also known as the **larynx** (LAR ingks), which is located behind your Adam's apple. The rushing air makes your vocal folds (also called vocal cords) vibrate. That vibration creates sound waves, which travel to your mouth.

But that's not the end of the story. If it were, a conversation between two friends who meet on the street might go like this:

Instead, the mouth takes these raw sounds and shapes them into the consonants and syllables that make up words. Almost all of the major players in your mouth—the lips, tongue, teeth, jaws, and others—get into the act. And if you doubt us. . .

Try this:

Say "Frank fell to Earth from Venus" without letting your upper teeth touch your lower lip.

Or "Daniel's tacos are obnoxious" without letting your tongue touch the roof of your mouth.

Or "Benjamin blew his tuba" without closing your mouth.

See what we mean?

A Couple of Really Deep Questions About Voices

Why are boys' voices (usually) deeper than girls' voices?

Boys tend to have bigger bodies than girls, so they also tend to have longer, thicker vocal folds. The longer and thicker a vocal fold is, the more slowly it vibrates, which produces a lower sound.

THE HARDER THEY FALL

When boys' voices become deeper, they fall about one octave (roughly eight notes). Girls' voices only drop down two or three notes.

Think of a pair of saxophones. A tenor saxophone produces a relatively high sound, while the larger baritone saxophone makes a deeper sound. Just keep in mind that sometimes boys can be tenor saxophones and girls can be baritone saxophones, and both can still sound totally cool.

Why do voices change as we age? And why is it so much more embarrassing when it happens to boys?

As you just read, thicker vocal folds produce deeper sounds. As you grow, your vocal folds thicken. In girls, though, the thickening is modest, and it happens gradually. But in boys, the vocal folds become much thicker. At first, the other body parts involved in producing a voice don't work well with this thick new vocal fold. Occasionally there's a screw-up and your nice, pleasant voice "breaks." This means just for a split second you sound like Minnie Mouse.

For some reason, voice breaks seem to happen to boys at the worst times, like when they're answering a question in class or trying to look cool in front of a girl. Smart alecks will laugh, but don't worry: Their turn will come.

Snoopy Syndrome
Periodontal (perry oh DON tull) disease, an infection of the gums, turns up in only one other species besides humans: beagles.

Why do some doctors make you say "ahhh" when they look in your mouth?

To improve the view. Doctors need to look around in the back of your mouth for signs of inflammation or infection. But your mouth is awfully crowded.

Using a wooden depressor (also known in the medical profession as an "ahhh stick"), the doctor holds down your big flabby tongue. But the roof of your mouth hangs down and blocks the view—until you say "ahhh." Then it raises up, letting the doctor see all.

If a doctor asks you to say "doe," "ray," and "me," he or she is probably looking for new members for the hospital glee club.

"Eeeeuw—
I Sound Like a Dork!"

It is a well-known fact that when people hear their voice on tape for the first time they almost always spaz out. They say that their voices sound nothing like the weird ones coming out of the tape player. They insist that the machine must be broken.

Well, the machine probably isn't broken, but your brain is acting a little tricky. Push the "record" button on the tape recorder and say a few words. If you can't think of anything to say, just recite the poem below:

An experiment for people who've been hearing strange voices—namely, their own.

What you need: A tape recorder, your voice.

Roses are red Violets are blue This poem doesn't rhyme Sorry about that.

Roses are red Violets are blue This poem doesn't rhyme Sorry about that.

After you've recorded your voice, try to imagine how you think you sound. Now play back the recording of your voice. Sounds a bit different, right?

Here's what happened: All sounds—including your voice played back on tape—travel through the air to your eardrum. Nerves in your eardrum vibrate, sending signals to the part of the brain that senses sound. But you don't hear the sound of your own voice with your eardrum. Your voice causes the bones in your skull to vibrate very slightly, and that vibration sends sound signals to your brain. Your skull bones are bigger and a different shape than your eardrum, so they deliver a very different message to the brain. The result: you hear two different voices.

If you like the way you sound on the tape, pack it up and mail it to a recording company, and maybe they'll make you the next singing superstar. And be sure to send your pals at Planet Dexter, tickets to your first big concert (two, on the aisle, please)!

THE ARENA
PRESENTS

The wonderfully talented

_____
WRITE YOUR NAME HERE

DRAW YOUR PICTURE OR
PASTE YOUR PHOTOGRAPH IN THIS SPACE

Fast Talking

SPEECH LIMIT 88 WPM*

*Words per Minute

If you call someone a "fast talker," that usually means you don't trust everything that person says. Fast talkers speak speedily because they hope others won't really hear what they're saying.

Well, some fast talkers, it turns out, really are just people who can talk fast. When they speak, wordsspill-outoftheirmouths so fast that you'd think their tongues might catch fire. Steve Woodmore, a man from England, claims to be the world's fastest talker. How fast does he talk? Well, consider this: When you speak normally, you probably say between 40 and 80 words per minute. If you try to read something aloud rapidly, you might be able to rattle off up to 200 words per minute. But Steve has been known to speak over 600 words per minute. With a nifty British accent, too!

Try this:

Here's a list of the presidents of the United States of America. Get a watch with a second hand and time how long it takes you to read aloud every name, going at a normal speed.

How did you do? Now read the list again, only this time say the names as fast as you can. No cheating—you have to pronounce every syllable so that someone else can understand it. Try to beat the time set by Nick Montelione, a teen from New York—he can name all the presidents in under 20 seconds!

Do You Dare Exceed the Speech Limit?

George Washington
John Adams
Thomas Jefferson
James Madison
James Monroe
John Quincy Adams
Andrew Jackson
Martin Van Buren
William H. Harrison
John Tyler
James Polk
Zachary Taylor
Millard Fillmore
Franklin Pierce

James Buchanan
Abraham Lincoln
Andrew Johnson
Ulysses S. Grant
Rutherford B. Hayes
James Garfield
Chester Alan Arthur
Grover Cleveland
Benjamin Harrison
Grover Cleveland
William McKinley
Theodore Roosevelt
William Howard Taft
Woodrow Wilson
Warren Harding

Calvin Coolidge
Herbert Hoover
Franklin D. Roosevelt
Harry Truman
Dwight Eisenhower
John F. Kennedy
Lyndon Johnson
Richard Nixon
Gerald Ford
Jimmy Carter
Ronald Reagan
George Bush
Bill Clinton

That's a Lot of Hot Air

You breathe in oxygen and exhale carbon dioxide through your nose and mouth. In a day you breathe in and out about 500 cubic feet of air—enough to blow up several thousand party balloons.

The Mechanics of Munching

The Crushing Truth of it All

Picture a large slice of pepperoni pizza (like the one below).

Now imagine a short length of garden hose (like the one out in your yard, only about six inches long). Now imagine making the pizza pass through one end of the hose and out the other. Squish! It would never fit.

Yet, your mouth has an amazing ability to make big hunks of food slide right down your own garden hose—that is, the tube in your neck that connects the back of your mouth to your stomach. You know it as your throat; doctors call it the pharynx (FAR ingks). This neat trick is chewing and swallowing, of course, and it goes like this:

After your canines and incisors tear off a chunk of food—like some of that pizza—it sits on the floor of your mouth. Instantly, it's attacked by saliva, which contains a substance called **amylase** (AM uh lace). Amylase begins to digest food while it's still in your mouth.

But food doesn't just sit there dissolving away. The tongue immediately starts pushing it around. It shoves the food into one corner, between the premolars and molars. Your lower jaw, called the **mandible** (MAN dih bull), moves up and down and side-to-side on a hinge, crushing food perched on the lower molars against the upper molars, which are attached to the upper jaw, known as the maxilla (MAKS ill ah). The cheek muscles flex to help keep the food in place. Then the tongue grabs the food and sweeps it over to the other set of molars so they can have a turn at bringing this hunk of pizza down to size.

When your mouth has done enough dissolving and chewing, the once delectable-looking hunk of pizza is nothing but a pale ball of mush known as a bolus (BOW luss). And it's ready to be sucked down the pharynx, to your stomach. After the bolus is whooshed away, you go to work on another bite of pizza.

DID YOU KNOW...

. . . that the ancient Greeks used to chew resin from the mastic tree, so it's no coincidence that a fancy word for chewing is mastication (mass tih KAY shun). Throughout history people have chewed on different types of tree sap. Turn the page to find out what you call that sticky stuff today.

43

Chewing Gum

Calisthenics for Your Jaws

Chewing gum as we know it today is made of a tree sap called chicle (CHIK ull) that comes from sapodilla trees, found only in Central and South America. (Another word for tree sap is latex—pronounced LAY teks.) Chicle is mixed with latex from other trees and artificial munchy material, plus sugar, coloring, and other ingredients to make everybody's favorite chewable treat.

Chewing gum, bubble gum—what's the difference?
A small difference that provides big results: the basic recipe for bubble gum includes latex similar to the kind that comes from a rubber tree. That makes the gum stretch more, allowing bigger bubbles to be blown.

Bubble gum is also pink, most of the time, but not for any special reason. That just happened to be the only color of dye the inventor of bubble gum had handy when he made his first batch, in 1928.

A Great Reason to Buy American!

In Japan, one popular chewing gum flavor is pickled plum.

ASK THE DR: EVERYONE KNOWS THAT YOU'RE SUPPOSED TO CHEW GUM—

NOT EAT IT. SO DOES THAT MEAN GUM IS NOT A FOOD?

The answer is no—sort of. The U.S. Food and Drug Administration, which makes sure the stuff you eat is safe, has a three-part definition of food: 1) stuff that humans and animals eat, 2) stuff used to make other stuff that humans and animals eat, and 3) chewing gum. In other words, no one is sure what to call chewing gum. So you could say that it's food, but there's no food quite like it.

BUT WHAT HAPPENS IF YOU DO SWALLOW YOUR GUM?

Nothing much. It won't stick to your stomach. But you won't digest it, either, since gum contains plant fibers your body can't break down. The gum will simply exit your body the way all food does, during a visit to the bathroom.

A Lot of Hot Air

One of the biggest bubble-gum bubbles on record was blown by a woman in California; it measured 22 inches across.

PPPffff!!!

Bite-Size Facts

Fill Up on These Tidbits about Infamous Chompers

The real Dracula didn't bite people on the neck. Or on the toes or fingers or backsides. In fact, the real Dracula wasn't even a vampire, which is supposedly a corpse that has returned to life and goes around biting people to suck out their blood. Bram Stoker, the author of the book *Dracula*, named his villain after an actual Romanian prince. Not that the real Dracula was a nice guy. He once ate a hearty meal while watching his enemies impaled on sharp stakes, and from time to time boiled peasants to death.

Play Dental Detective

What you need: A pack of chewing gum (in the stick form, preferably sugarless), a plate or paper towel, three friends.

And you can quit worrying about getting bitten by werewolves, too.

They don't exist. Or at least they aren't the fanged, blood-thirsty types you see in movies. There is a form of mental illness that makes people think that they've turned into wolves. They imagine that their faces have turned furry and that they've grown huge fangs. Some even howl at the moon. But they tend not to be biters.

Crime does not pay—especially if you can't keep your teeth to yourself.

Several notorious murderers have been convicted, in part, because they bit their victims. The police were able to make an impression from the bite mark and match it to the suspect's teeth.

Biting does not pay—in the boxing ring.

Boxer Mike Tyson lost a championship bout and a lot of money in 1997 because he bit his opponent's ear—twice. The bitten boxer, Evander Holyfield, could have become very sick from Tyson's toothy attack; Doctor Saul tells you why.

When Man Bites Man

Fido may have bigger fangs, but your bite is usually worse (assuming Fido has had his rabies shots). The bacteria in your mouth can cause serious infections if it gets into another person's bloodstream.

Give each of your friends a stick of gum and leave the room. While you're away, have each one unwrap his or her gum and gently bite into it the long way—just hard enough to make an impression with his or her teeth.

Then have your friends put their gum on the plate, in no special order. When you return to the room, make your friends open their mouths. Study their teeth. Can you match the bite marks to your friends' teeth?

Oral, But Not

People Do Some Pretty Bizarre Things with

Pica (PIE kuh) is a craving to eat things that don't really qualify as food, unless you're a goat. A list of things that people afflicted with pica have been known to eat includes dirt, clay, chalk, glue, and hair.

Some people have to eat dirt to get important minerals that their diet doesn't provide. Eating dirt is called **geophagy** (jee OFF uh jee).

When people eat like cows—literally—they're said to have **rumination** (roo mih NAY shun) disorder. Sufferers regurgitate their food, which means they force it back up from their stomach and into their mouths. Then they chew the food a second time and swallow. Cattle, goats, deer, camels and some other animals, known as **ruminants** (ROO mih nintz) do the same thing, only they must do it to survive. Ruminating allows an animal to digest the fibers in grass and plants.

AND ACCORDING TO THE GUINNESS BOOK OF WORLD RECORDS. . .

Normal

Their Mouths

. . . a man in England recited the lyrics of Queen's album, *A Night at the Opera*, backwards in under 10 minutes.

. . . a Belgian man once lifted over 600 pounds with his teeth.

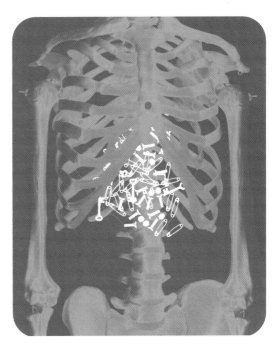

. . . a Canadian woman who was a compulsive swallower gobbled up 2,533 non-food objects, including 947 bent pins.

. . . a woman in Northern Ireland screamed the word

" QUIET "

at 121.7 decibels. And a British man whistled even louder. Both sounds are much louder than a jack hammer.

. . . a man from Armenia once pulled two railroad cars 23 feet using nothing but his teeth.

Oral Exam

How Mouth-Smart Are You?

Human mouths can develop or indicate some pretty strange, even serious problems. See if you can sort out the real oral oddities from the ones we made up. Check off the ones that you think are real.

1
- [ ] a. Grinner's disorder: The muscles in your face become paralyzed in the shape of a smile.

OR

- [ ] b. Tourette's syndrome: A sickness that causes the sufferer to grimace, grunt, bark, or even swear uncontrollably.

2
- [ ] a. Strawberry tongue: The little bumps on your tongue become swollen and red. A sign of scarlet fever.

OR

- [ ] b. Banana tongue: Your tongue curls slightly and develops a yellow coating. Found in malaria patients.

3
- [ ] a. Dexterous. The ability to pull one's upper lip over one's head while pulling one's lower lip over one's feet, so that in a matter of minutes, one's totally eaten oneself.

OR

- [ ] b. Lison's case. Refers to a dental patient in France, who in 1896 was determined to have grown not just the normal second set of teeth, but also a third and fourth set of teeth.

4
- [ ] a. Thrush: An infection caused by a fungus that makes white spots grow on your mouth and tongue.

OR

- [ ] b. Parrot: A mental disorder that makes you repeat what other people say.

5

a Furrowed gums: A deep dent in the gums, left by too-tight braces.

OR

b Trench mouth: An infection that makes your gums bleed and gives you stinky breath.

6

a Brother Giovanni Battista Orsenigo, a dentist of Rome, Italy, who from 1868 to 1904, saved all the teeth he extracted from patients. His collection of 2,000,744 teeth filled three huge crates.

OR

b Sister Aloha Alfonso "Smitty" Dexter, of Bass Bite Creek, Montana, who, in 1903, composed and first performed the timeless classic, "All I Want for July 4th Are My Two Front Teeth."

7

a Bald tongue: The little bumps on your tongue temporarily shrink, giving it a smooth feel.

OR

b Hairy tongue: The little bumps on your tongue temporarily grow, which makes your mouth feel like you're eating a wig.

8

a Geographic tongue: Your tongue develops white patches shaped like countries on a map.

OR

b Geologic tongue: A hardening of the skin, or epithelium, that covers the tongue.

ANSWERS

1. B; 2. A; 3. B; 4. A; 5. B; 6. A; 7. B; 8. A.

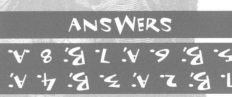

51

Fire in the Hole!

Chili Peppers, the Mouth's Most

Another peculiar, but very popular, oral tradition is eating chili peppers. Chilies have an ingredient that makes them taste hot. Some chili peppers are really, really hot. So hot that when you bite into one you feel like a small volcano just erupted in your mouth. Your mouth hurts so much that you're usually speechless. If you can talk at all, you can say only one word:

Yeeeeeeow!

The hottest type of chili pepper is called the **habañero** (ah bahn YAYR o). It's yellowish-orange and it's name means "Havana-like," which may be because the habañero comes from the city in Cuba by the same name, where it can get pretty steamy. But not as hot as an *habañero*.

Greetings from HAVANA

Try this: If you have some Tabasco sauce in the refrigerator, pour a little onto a spoon and taste it. Think it's pretty hot stuff? Well chew on this: an *habañero* is 66 times hotter!

(Don't gulp down water or any other cold beverage to put out the flames of a hot chili pepper—that seems to make the pain worse. Eating bread or rice will soothe the flames, though.)

A PAINFUL QUESTION

If chili peppers burn your mouth so badly, why do so many people like eating them? No one knows for sure. Some people like to take risks in life, and eating super-scalding peppers may seem like a way to act risky, but not get seriously hurt. After all, even though you feel like flames are leaping off your lips, the pain goes away a minute or two after eating a chili pepper. Some

Macho Menace

doctors think, though, that there's a secret ingredient in chili peppers that releases brain chemicals that make some people feel happy.

Prescription: Peppers

The stuff that makes chili peppers scorching hot is a substance called capsaicin (cap SAY uh sin). Weirdly enough, capsaicin is also used to make medication to relieve certain types of pain. A scientist figured out that even though eating chilies hurts at first, if you eat enough of them the capsaicin eventually turns off the nerves that feel pain. That makes your tongue numb. Now people who have achy bones and joints take pills with capsaicin, and that numbs their pain.

HOT CUISINE

The Aztecs, who lived in Mexico until the 1500s, put chili peppers in everything they ate—including chocolate.

No Peppers With My Cheese, Please

Most animals hate hot peppers. Sometimes workers cover underground cables with capsaicin to keep rats from gnawing on them.

53

Mighty UNUSUAL Mouths

A Look Inside the Amazing and Often Very Strange Jowls of a Few Members of the Animal Kingdom

Be careful if a beaver ever offers to kiss your hand. Their incisors are like chisels. Beavers chew twice as hard as humans. It takes a typical eager beaver just five minutes to gnaw through a thin tree. In one year, its choppers can bring down up to 300 trees.

Gnaw-ty Mouths

Talk about getting a lot of fiber in your diet! Actually, beavers only snack on a little bark here and there—most of the wood they gnaw on is inedible. To keep from swallowing wood splinters, beavers have special flaps in the backs of their mouths. When they want to eat and drink, the flaps relax.

It doesn't happen very often, but if a beaver breaks an incisor, it usually dies. Here's why: Say a beaver busts an upper incisor. That means its incisor on his lower jaw has nothing to click against.

Unlike human teeth, beaver teeth keep growing. Eventually, that lower incisor grows so much that it circles back into the beaver's mouth and makes it impossible for the beaver to swallow food. Eventually, it starves.

Chomp! And Don't Forget to Write!

Beaver moms need to make room in their dens when they have new babies. So a mom kicks out her older children by biting them.

Dear Mom,

I miss you even though you bit me. Today I gnawed three trees. Please come visit soon.

Love, Billy

An Egg-Stremely Mouthy Fish

Cichlids

(SIK lidz) are a kind of freshwater fish found in many parts of the world. Certain varieties of cichlids are also called mouth brooders. That's because after a mother cichlid lays its eggs, she keeps them in her mouth. Even after the eggs hatch, the tiny cichlids spend most of their time hanging around inside the mother's mouth, especially if there's another fish around who might like to eat them. Eventually, the mother fish gets tired of the living arrangement and stops letting the little cichlids back in after they've gone out to play. Then it's time for them to live on their own.

IT SMELLS WITH FORKED TONGUE

You've already read that humans "taste" food with their noses. Well, lizards do things a little differently: They smell with their mouths.

A lizard has a pair of compartments in the front of its mouth called Jacobson's organs. These organs are wired directly to the part of a lizard's brain that's responsible for identifying smells. When a lizard jabs out its tongue, it's "tasting" the air. Air particles stick to the tongue, which it then sucks back into its mouth and presses against the Jacobson's organs. Lizards that have tongues shaped like a two-pronged fork are the best smellers of all, because they can insert the air particles they lapped up all the way into the Jacobson's organs.

Lots of animals don't have teeth. The largest beast alive, the blue whale, doesn't have a single tooth in its enormous head. But it doesn't need them, since it doesn't chew its food. Like certain other whales, the Big Blue sifts tiny shrimps and other microscopic sea creatures out of the water using fringes on the bony plates in its mega mouth. Then it simply swallows them whole.

Turtles have strong jaws, but no teeth. Birds don't have choppers, either. Instead of mashing their food with molars, they have a special pouch called a gizzard (rhymes with "wizard") in their stomachs that grinds food before they can digest it. Earthworms have gizzards, too.

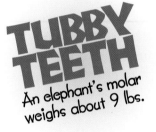

TUBBY TEETH
An elephant's molar weighs about 9 lbs.

The Scoop on Pelican Mouths

A poet once wrote, "A wonderful bird is a pelican/His bill will hold more than his belican." And it's true. Pelicans have fleshy pouches attached to their bottom bills. Some pelicans have such big pouches that they scoop up as much as three gallons of water every time they dip their bills into the ocean in search of food. (Fortunately, they spit out most of the water, or else they might explode.) On hot days, pelicans lie around and fan themselves with their fleshy flaps.

Can You Stomach This!

Starfish: The Foulest Mouths of All

Never, ever have lunch with a starfish. Not even if the starfish offers to pay. The gross-out won't be worth it—starfish have possibly the foulest mouths on the planet.

A typical starfish meal goes like this: It wanders along the ocean floor looking for an oyster. When it finds one, the starfish grabs the shell and wrestles it open. Next, the starfish opens wide and out pops its stomach! Really! The starfish turns its stomach inside out and shoots the big, fleshy mess out of its mouth to surround the oyster meat. Digestive juices on the stomach turn the meat into mush and then **SLURP!**—the starfish sucks down the oyster (without any cocktail sauce!).

And if you think that's a revolting sight, you really wouldn't want to stick around when the meal is done. After all, some starfish don't have a certain body part that's designed specifically to, um, eliminate waste products from the body. If you know what we mean. So, they poop and pee ... through their mouths!

YUK-O

The Yawning of a New Era
They're Not What You Think

Scientists aren't sure why, but yawning seems to be contagious.

Mark our words. . .
Some day a know-it-all will tell you that it is a scientific fact that you yawn because your brain needs oxygen. And when they do, you can yawn right in their face and say something incredibly clever like, "Conventional wisdom bores me—especially when it's WRONG!"

In fact, no one is really sure why we yawn. According to the old theory, yawning was a sign that your blood had too much carbon dioxide in it, so you needed to balance the mix with a big gulp of oxygen. You take in oxygen every time you inhale. But scientists proved that you get much more oxygen into your body simply by breathing normally. So the yawning mystery continues.

It's perfectly normal to yawn at any time of day, but people seem to do it more often when they're bored or tired.

But did you know that a lot of people yawn when they're nervous? The tradition of putting your hand over your mouth while you yawn may come from an ancient superstition: People used to believe that the devil could enter your mouth during a yawn, so it was important to protect yourself. Today, it's just considered good manners not to show off your molars every time you yawn.

Try this: The next time you're in a room full of people, let loose a big, mouth-stretching yawn. Then wait. Does anyone else yawn? If so, it's no coincidence. Scientists aren't sure why, but yawning seems to be contagious.

A WEARY WARRIOR
The Apache warrior known as Geronimo was called another name by his own people: Goyathlay, which in English means "one who yawns"

Metal Mouths

Straight Talk About Tin Grins

Q: What do you call someone whose only friends have absolutely perfect teeth?

A: Lonely! But while few of us have movie-star smiles, some people's teeth are really less than perfect. They've got a malocclusion (mal oh CLUE shun), which means "bad bite." To see if you have a malocclusion, look in a mirror. Bite down and bare your teeth, like a mad dog. Do the upper and lower rows of teeth line up evenly? If not, blame your jaws. When a jaw is too small, sometimes your teeth try to grow in, but don't fit. They push and shove one another, and grow in crooked. People with "buck" teeth have a jaw that's too short, which leaves the upper teeth sticking out. If you have a long jaw, your lower teeth will stick out too much, a look known as a "bulldog" mouth.

A malocclusion can make chewing and speaking difficult. Fortunately, a dentist called an orthodontist can fix a bad bite. Unfortunately, the solution is the dreaded B-word: Braces.

Braces have been around since at least 1000 B.C., when some Greeks wore them. Today's are made of metal or ceramic brackets, wires, and springs. The brackets get cemented to the teeth. The wires are threaded through the brackets and push or pull the teeth. Orthodontists also stretch rubber bands from one tooth to another sometimes.

All this machinery in your mouth might sound cool. But braces can hurt a bit, especially at first. Even after you get used to them, you have to get them tightened every month or so, and that means more discomfort. Still, nobody has to wear braces forever, although some people have kept theirs on for up to twenty years. Two or three years is about the average.

On the plus side, some orthodontists let you choose wild-colored rubber bands, like pink or fluorescent green. Some people grow to love their colorful new mouths.

Not For Kids Only

One fourth of all people with braces are adults.

Ask the Big Mouth: If two metal mouths kiss, can their braces lock together? Probably not, since to do it the kissers would have to rub their teeth together. However, people who wear braces say kissing can hurt, since the inside of their lips press against the metal. Some orthodontists offer covers that slip over braces, protecting your lips. If you want one, but don't think your smooching habits are any of your orthodontist's business, tell him or her you play tuba in the school band.

Chuckles

And How to Crack Up a Chimpanzee

And last, but not least, the very best things you can do with your mouth.

SMiLE! Wide as you can. Hold it. Just one more second... and, relax.

Phew! After that workout, your zygomaticus muscles must be pooped.

Zygo-who?

Zygomaticus (zie go MAT tik kuss) major muscles. You've got two, one in each cheek. When you smile, the zygomaticus major muscles hoist up the corners of your mouth to make that familiar and pleasant facial expression.

Laughing is even better exercise. It takes fifteen facial muscles to roar with laughter, so you get a good workout just by watching a funny movie. In fact, the old saying that "Laughter is the best medicine" isn't as silly as it sounds. Scientists once discovered that while people watch comedy shows their bodies make extra white blood cells, which help keep you from getting sick.

Getting lots of laughs also makes your heart stronger and helps blood flow throughout your body with greater ease.

Have you ever GiGGLED so hard you felt weak? That's because laughter makes most of your muscles relax. Be grateful, though, for a muscle known as the vesical sphincter (VESS ih kull SFINK ter). It doesn't relax when you laugh. If it did, you would pee in your pants.

It's a good idea not to take a drink of anything when a funny person is cracking jokes. When you laugh, air comes rushing out of your throat. If there happens to be liquid in your throat at the time, the air forces it all the way up into your nasal

and Grins

passage. And there's nothing more embarrassing than having milk come out your nose.

Humans aren't the only laughers in the animal kingdom. Chimpanzees love to yuk it up. The best way to make a chimp laugh is to chase it around. (A chimp comedy club would be one very chaotic place.)

The spotted, or "laughing," hyena (high EE nah) is a creature that looks like a big dog (but is actually more closely related to the cat) and lives in Africa. Laughing hyenas get their nickname from their wild, whooping-it-up bark. Hyenas laugh when they're excited or looking for a date with another hyena. Which isn't so different from humans, since women are always saying they like men with a good sense of humor.

HA HA Hey, Baby! Whadda ya doin' Friday night?

You began laughing when you were about four months old. And if you're lucky, you'll never stop. At least not for long. The folks at Planet Dexter hope this book helped you exercise both your brain and your zygomaticus muscles. And if you haven't yet, maybe the next page will help. . . .

THE LAUGH TEST: A BATTLE OF WITS

Laughter can be contagious, and TV producers know it. A lot of comedy shows on TV use a "laugh track." That's a tape recording of people cracking up in hysterics. Next time you watch a comedy show with a laugh track . . .

TRY THIS: Figure out how funny the show really is.

What you need: A pencil and paper; some friends.

While you watch the show, tally the number of jokes by scoring one point every time the laugh track plays.

Meanwhile, keep track of your friends' laughter. Score one point if anyone in the room laughs at a joke, even if it's just a giggle.

When the show is over add up each total. To figure out the show's Level of Actual Funniness (LAF) score, use this formula:

HA HA HA
Friend's Laughs ÷ Laugh Track Laughs = Level of Actual Funniness

Use this system with your favorite comedy shows to figure out which one is truly the funniest.

Try Solving These Riddles

But keep one thing in mind: We only meant them to be tongue-in-cheek.

Which basketball star never gets tired of drills?
Dentist Rodman

What did one uvula say to the other?
Lately, I've been feeling a little down in the mouth.

What famous preacher is always mouthing off about something?
Oral Roberts

What do you say to a seal who talks too much?
Quit being such a blubber mouth.

And what would you expect him to say in response?
Okay—my lips are sealed.

Who was the Chinese leader who licked all of his opponents?
Mao Tse Tongue

Zeke's mother washed out his mouth out with soap after he talked back to her. How do you think this made Zeke feel?
He must have been angry, because he was really foaming at the mouth.

Blah blah blah

Why did Picasso rinse his mouth out with turpentine?

He wanted to cleanse his palate.

What movie funny man has rotten teeth?
Jim Caries

What did one lip say to the other?
I sure am tired of getting smacked around.

What should you say to someone whose mouth is frozen shut?
Keep a stiff upper lip.

How did the cowboy know the oats he served his stallion were yummy?
He heard it from the horse's mouth.

Name the book in which a handsome photographer travels to the Midwest to take pictures of people's teeth:
The Bridgework of Madison County

What did the premolar say to the incisor?
"I'd drop by to visit, but I'm afraid to walk past that canine."

Who's the rat who always has a big wide grin?
M-I-C-K-E-Y
M-O-U-T-H

More Tasty Books from Planet Dexter

Grossology
The Science of Really Gross Things!
by Sylvia Branzei

Yup: It's slimy, oozy, stinky, smelly stuff explained. *Grossology* features the gag-rageous science behind the body's most disgusting functions: Burps, vomit, scabs, ear wax, you name it. Who could ask for anything more?

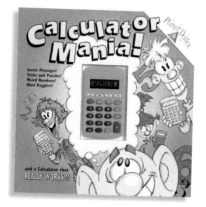

Calculator Mania!
by The Editors of Planet Dexter

We give you a cool calculator and a bunch of ideas for playing with it and—oops!—learning a little something about numbers and math along the way. Incorporates lots of games and an unforgettable strategy for getting rich quick.

Planet Ant
by The Editors of Planet Dexter

This amazing book includes ant planet, sand, and an ants-by-mail coupon (not prepaid). Learn all about the anty kingdom while getting to know your new companions.